TO MY DAUGHTERS, CLAUDIA AND CLAIRE,

WHO, DESPITE THE RISK, HAVE ALWAYS BRAVELY SUPPORTED

ME IN MY OWN QUEST TO REACH THE STARS — M. K.

TO THE ASTRONAUTS OF NASA WHO GIVE US THE CREATIVE ENERGY TO

REACH FOR THE STARS — C. F. P.

SIMON & SCHUSTER BOOKS FOR YOUNG READERS
An imprint of Simon & Schuster Children's Publishing Division
1230 Avenue of the Americas, New York, New York 10020
Text copyright © 2012 by Mark Kelly
Illustrations copyright © 2012 by C. F. Payne
All rights reserved, including the right of reproduction in whole or in part in any form.
SIMON & SCHUSTER BOOKS FOR YOUNG READERS is a trademark of Simon & Schuster, Inc.
For information about special discounts for bulk purchases, please contact Simon & Schuster Special Sales at 1-866-506-1949 or business@simonandschuster.com.
The Simon & Schuster Speakers Bureau can bring authors to your live event. For more information or to book an event, contact the Simon & Schuster Speakers Bureau at 1-866-248-3049 or visit our website at www.simonspeakers.com.
Book design by Lucy Ruth Cummins
The text for this book is set in Gotham.
The illustrations for this book are rendered in mixed media.
Manufactured in China
0718 SCP
12 14 16 18 20 19 17 15 13
Library of Congress Cataloging-in-Publication Data
Kelly, Mark E.
Mousetronaut / Mark Kelly ; illustrated by C. F. Payne. —1st ed.
p. cm.
Summary: A small, but plucky, mouse named Meteor is sure that he can help the space shuttle astronauts, and ends up saving the whole mission.
Includes bibliographical references.
ISBN 978-1-4424-5824-6 (hardcover : alk. paper)
ISBN 978-1-4424-5832-1 (eBook)
1. Mice—Juvenile fiction. 2. Space shuttles—Juvenile fiction. 3. Astronauts—Juvenile fiction. [1. Mice—Fiction. 2. Space shuttles—Fiction. 3. Astronauts—Fiction.]
I. Payne, C. F., ill. II. Title.
PZ7.K296395Mou 2012
813.6—dc23
2012008497

MOUSETRONAUT

BASED ON A (PARTIALLY) TRUE STORY

ASTRONAUT MARK KELLY

ILLUSTRATED BY C. F. PAYNE

A PAULA WISEMAN BOOK

SIMON & SCHUSTER BOOKS FOR YOUNG READERS

New York London Toronto Sydney New Delhi

The space shuttle is set for a launch, and the astronauts are doing their last-minute training to prepare for the mission.

NASA is sending along some special guests for this flight,
and they're training too!

One mouse is smaller than all the rest. His name is Meteor. The other mice know he won't be chosen for this important mission.

But someone has his eye on Meteor, and he's impressed with the little mouse's hard work.

The Shuttle Commander announces that six mice will be selected for the flight. He picks five of the biggest, strongest mice.

But for the sixth spot, to everyone's surprise, he chooses . . .

Meteor!

All six are taken to their new home, a special cage called the Mouse Hotel! The other mice are nervous as the countdown begins. But not Meteor!

TEN—
NINE—
EIGHT—
SEVEN—
SIX—
FIVE—
FOUR—
THREE—
TWO—
ONE

At first the mice are pressed flat against their cages by the power of the launch.

But then the pressure goes away. The other mice cling to their cage in terror.

But not Meteor! He loves the feeling of weightlessness!

"Hey, little guy," the commander says. "You're a natural. A real live . . . mousetronaut!"

Meteor is taken from his cage and gets a tour of the shuttle. He can even see the Earth way off in the distance.

The astronauts are all very busy during the fourteen-day flight. There are space walks to take, and experiments to conduct.

But what can Meteor do to help?

Then, while answering e-mail, one of the astronauts notices the key to the control panel stuck between the monitors.

When he tries to get it out, it accidentally gets wedged farther down.

"This isn't good,"
says the commander.
"We need that key
back."

One astronaut tries to move the monitor.
It doesn't budge.

Another slips her
fingers into the crack,
but the key is stuck down
too deep.

One even tries pushing it out with a
long piece of metal, but with no luck.
No one can reach it.

The astronauts are getting worried. But as they discuss the problem, a tiny figure has an idea.

"Being the smallest isn't a bad thing," Meteor says to himself. "Maybe I *can* be useful on this flight."

Meteor squeezes his way
into the crack. The space
is dark and cramped, but
Meteor spots the key and
tugs at it with all his might.

"Hey! Look at what
our tiny friend has done,"
the commander says.
"He's saved
the mission!"

When the shuttle returns to Earth, Meteor is declared a hero. He's even given a brand-new uniform, and an official title—Mousetronaut!

All the astronauts cheer and applaud, but Meteor is already thinking about his next big mission!

AFTERWORD

I flew with mice during my first flight on space shuttle *Endeavour*. Just as NASA takes care with its human astronauts, animals are treated with consideration for their needs. Special cages were constructed with mesh that the mice could grip with their toes. Pressurized water containers and compressed food were installed and a waste containment system was created to keep things clean. During my first flight in 2001, there were eighteen mice on board. All of them, with one exception, clung to the inside of the mesh during the entire mission. One mouse, smaller than the rest, seemed to enjoy the experience and effortlessly floated around the cage. The story of *Mousetronaut* is inspired by that mission. We all watched him as he enjoyed the feeling of being weightless. I started to think about that mouse and what it would be like to have him as part of our crew. That real mouse stayed in the research cage through the mission, but he is what I based this story on. That experience is the partially true part of this story.

For most of human existence, people have longed to overcome the pull of gravity and fly above the Earth. This remained just a dream until December 17, 1903, when the Wright Brothers launched the first manned airplane, the *Flyer*, and challenged the birds for a place in the skies. That first flight lasted only 12 seconds, rising to a height of 20 feet and covering a distance of 120 feet. In the following years, faster and more sophisticated planes were developed and air travel flourished.

The idea that space travel was a distant dream changed in 1957 when the Soviet Union launched *Sputnik*, the first artificial satellite, into orbit around the Earth. The United States was determined to catch up and surpass the Soviets in outer space as well as on Earth. Both nations were in a competition to prove which was more powerful. The race into space had begun. Schools challenged students to work harder in science and math, and more money was put into education and research. In 1958 Congress created NASA, the National Aeronautics and Space Administration. In 1961 President Kennedy committed to have a man on the moon by the end of the decade. Many people thought this was impossible—too dangerous, too complicated, and too expensive. However, this goal was achieved and, on July 20, 1969, the United States won the race to the moon! Neil Armstrong and Buzz Aldrin became the first men to walk on the moon. They planted a flag and left a plaque that read HERE MEN FROM THE PLANET EARTH FIRST SET FOOT ON THE MOON JULY 1969 A.D. WE CAME IN PEACE FOR ALL MANKIND. The ingenuity, persistence, and courage of many people had turned what had been science fiction fantasy into reality.

In 1981 NASA launched the space shuttle, the first reusable spacecraft. Prior to the shuttle, spacecraft did not survive more than one voyage and the costs were becoming prohibitive. The shuttle was built to be used multiple times and designed with three main components: the orbiter that transports crew and cargo, two booster rockets, and a fuel tank. While both boosters and fuel tank are jettisoned during liftoff, the boosters are recoverable. The only part not reusable, the external fuel tank, burns up after liftoff and the pieces fall into the Pacific Ocean. The shuttle, which takes off like a rocket, lands like an airplane with the orbiter gliding onto a runway. On the launchpad, the space shuttle stands about 185 feet high (picture thirty-two men standing on top of one another) and, with a full payload and fully fueled, weighs about 4.5 million pounds.

The space shuttles flew for thirty years. When the program ended in July 2011, its fleet had grown to include five orbiters: *Atlantis*, *Challenger*, *Columbia*, *Discovery*, and *Endeavour*. All the orbiters were named after historical ships of exploration. *Endeavour* was named after Captain James Cook's famous ship that made voyages of discovery to Australia and New Zealand in the late 1700s. The name was selected in a competition by schoolchildren.

The space shuttles have flown 306 men and 49 women from 16 different countries during 135 missions, racking up over 537,114,016 miles—the equivalent of over 21,500 times around the Earth at a speed of about 17,500 mph. In 2010 it cost about $775 million for each space shuttle mission. The cost for the entire program was about $113.7 billion. The space shuttle helped build the International Space Station, transported and repaired satellites, deployed and serviced the Hubble Space Telescope, and conducted leading-edge experiments.

Travel in space is not for the fainthearted. Zero gravity, maintaining an adequate air supply, and cramped quarters are among the challenges the astronauts face. To qualify for a place on a space shuttle mission, a military background or advanced degrees in science, engineering, or medicine are important. In addition, astronauts must undergo rigorous training. The crew practices in simulated environments that replicate the conditions in space and take survival courses that require them to cope with unexpected emergencies. They have to learn how to live and maneuver in zero gravity, where they and everything on board are weightless and apt to float around unless tethered or strapped in. They have to learn how to go to the bathroom in space and how to eat and sleep in space.

Since water doesn't flow like it does on Earth, the astronauts clean themselves with wet wipes or washcloths—one with liquid soap and a wet one to rinse. They can use special products that scientists have created for space travel such as foamless soap that doesn't require water. They use dry shampoo for their hair and swallow their toothpaste (*ugh*). They go to the bathroom on toilets that use flowing air instead of water. Waste products are stored in the spaceship and disposed of after landing. They have special exercise machines to help them keep in shape: a floating treadmill, special weights, and exercise bikes. Their diet includes over 400 different meals, snacks, and drinks. Some are freeze-dried and water has to be added. Solid food is also available and magnets are used to keep forks and knives from floating off the table. When they are not busy working, the astronauts can read or play games or communicate with friends and family and even schoolchildren by e-mail or video links.

Astronauts are not the only travelers in space. In fact, they were not the first. The earliest space travelers were animals. Scientists wanted to see the effects of weightlessness before sending people into space. Fruit flies were the first to be sent. Mice and monkeys soon followed, although these flights only reached suborbital altitudes. In 1957 Laika, a dog, became the first animal actually sent into orbit. She was launched into space by the Soviets on *Sputnik II*. Although Laika did not survive the flight, she captured the attention of the world. In 1959 two monkeys, Abel and Baker, were carried in the nose cone of an American Jupiter missile to a 300-mile altitude. They returned to Earth successfully.

In 1961 a chimpanzee named Ham became the first chimp in space. More than a passenger, Ham had a mission. Could he perform the tasks he had been trained for on Earth while traveling thousands of miles per hour in space? Would he be able to push a lever on cue? He would and he could! After his service, Ham retired to the National Zoo in Washington, D.C., where he lived for the rest of his life. Arabella and Anita, two spiders, also took an active part on their flight. These spiders were part of a Skylab mission experiment, suggested by a high school student, to find out if spiders would be able to spin webs in near-weightlessness. It turns out they can, and that the webs they spun in space were similar to their webs on Earth. Along with the monkeys, chimps, dogs, and spiders, other nonhuman voyagers included a cat, assorted turtles, Japanese tree frogs, roundworms, tardigrades, insects, rats, and, of course, mice.

Our mouse had the right stuff . . . he was a Mousetronaut.

TO LEARN MORE · Bibliography

Aldrin, Buzz. *Look to the Stars*. New York: G. P. Putnam's Sons, 2009.

Barchers, Suzanne I. *Revolution in Space*. New York: Marshall Cavendish Benchmark, 2010.

Bredeson, Carmen. *What Do Astronauts Do?* Berkeley Heights, NJ: Enslow, 2008.

Chaikin, Andrew. *Mission Control, This Is Apollo: The Story of the First Voyages to the Moon*. New York: Penguin Group, 2009.

Floca, Brian. *Moonshot: The Flight of Apollo 11*. New York: Atheneum Books for Young Readers, 2008.

McCarthy, Meghan. *Astronaut Handbook*. New York: Alfred A. Knopf, 2008.

McNulty, Faith. *If You Decide to Go to the Moon*. New York: Scholastic, 2005.

Ross, Stewart. *Moon: Science, History, and Mystery*. New York: Scholastic, 2009.

Skurzynski, Gloria. *This Is Rocket Science: True Stories of the Risk-taking Scientists Who Figure Out Ways to Explore Beyond Earth*. Washington, DC: National Geographic, 2010.

Space: A Visual Encyclopedia. London: New York: Dorling Kindersley Limited, 2010.

Thimmesh, Catherine. *Team Moon: How 400,000 People Landed Apollo 11 on the Moon*. Boston: Houghton Mifflin Company, 2006.

Internet Resources: *Many of these sites have videos or interactive games.*

NASA nasa.gov

NASA History of Animals in Space
history.nasa.gov/animals.html

NASA Space Shuttle
nasa.gov/shuttle

NASA for Students
www.nasa.gov/audience/forstudents

NASA Science for Kids
nasascience.nasa.gov/kids

About.com: Space/Astronomy: space.about
.com/cs/spaceshuttles/a/bathroominspace.htm

Amazing Space amazing-space.stsci.edu

Astronomy for Kids kidsastronomy.com

ESA (European Space Agency): Lessons Online:
Human Spaceflight and Exploration
esa.int/esaMI/Lessons_online/
SEMF1FXRA0G_0.html

Kidsites.com
kidsites.com/sites-edu

Space-Age Living: Building the International
Space Station school.discoveryeducation
.comschooladventures/spacestation

Space Camp spacecamp.com

Space Place spaceplace.nasa.gov